POCKETFUL OF NONSENSE

By James Marshall

AN ARTISTS AND WRITERS GUILD BOOK
Golden Books
Western Publishing Company, Inc.
850 Third Avenue, New York, New York 10022

Library of Congress Cataloging-in-Publication Data

Pocketful of nonsense/ [compiled and illustrated] by James Marshall.
p.   cm.
Summary: Old favorites and original works by Marshall make up this collection of humorous rhymes, limericks, and poems.
ISBN 0-307-17552-9 : $12.95 ($16.95 Can.)
1. Children's poetry. 2. Nonsense verses. 3. Limericks. Juvenile. [1. Humorous poetry. 2. Poetry–Collections.]
I. Marshall, James, 1942-1992
PN6109.97.P62   1993
398.8–dc20
93-18297
CIP
AC

Table of Contents

Fuzzy Wuzzy was a bear,
Fuzzy Wuzzy had no hair.
Fuzzy Wuzzy wasn't fuzzy,
was he?

There was a young man of Bengal
who went to a fancy-dress ball.
He went, just for fun,
dressed up as a bun,
and a dog ate him up in the hall.

There was an old man of Blackheath
who sat on his set of false teeth.
    Said he with a start,
    "Oh Lord, bless my heart!
I've bitten myself underneath!"

Jack Hall,
he is so small
a mouse could eat him,
hat and all.

12

Cinderella,
dressed in yella,
went upstairs
to kiss her fella,
made a mistake and kissed a snake.
How many doctors did it take?

A porker from East Chutney, Wales,
bespattered his top hat and tails.
   Now bear this in mind
    that clothes make the swine,
but mudbaths are good for what ails.
—J.M.

A tomcat in fine tenor voice
sang out in the church of his choice,
  "When the service is through
  I will dine on mouse stew.
For this I do truly rejoice."
  —J.M.

A peanut sat on a railroad track.
His heart was all a-flutter.
The five-fifteen came rushing by—
toot! toot! Peanut butter!

Through the teeth and past the gums— look out, stomach, here it comes!

A bulldog was watching his weight.
He watched and he watched while he ate.
"It defies understanding
why I keep expanding,"
he said as he licked clean his plate.
—J.M.

A gentleman dining at Crewe
found quite a large mouse in his stew.
    Said the waiter, "Don't shout
    and wave it about,
or the rest will be wanting one, too!"

I love you, I love you,
I love you divine.
Please give me your bubble gum—
you're *sitting* on mine!

Get up, get up, you lazy head.
Get up, you lazy sinner.
We need those sheets for tablecloths.
It's nearly time for dinner.

Antoinette Leach came in from the beach
with a lobster asleep in her curls.
    Said her mother, "My dear,
    it's perfectly clear,
you're simply not like other girls."
                    —J.M.

A sinister spider named Ruth
set up a photography booth.
    In clever disguise
    she'd lure juicy flies
who too late would discover the truth.
—J.M.

There was an old man of Peru
who dreamed he was eating his shoe.
   He woke in the night
   in a terrible fright
and found it was perfectly true.

There was a young man of Devizes
whose ears were of different sizes.
    The one that was small
    was no use at all,
but the other won several prizes.

A horse and a flea and three blind mice
sat on a curbstone shooting dice.
The horse he slipped and fell on the flea.
The flea said, "Whoops, there's a horse on me."

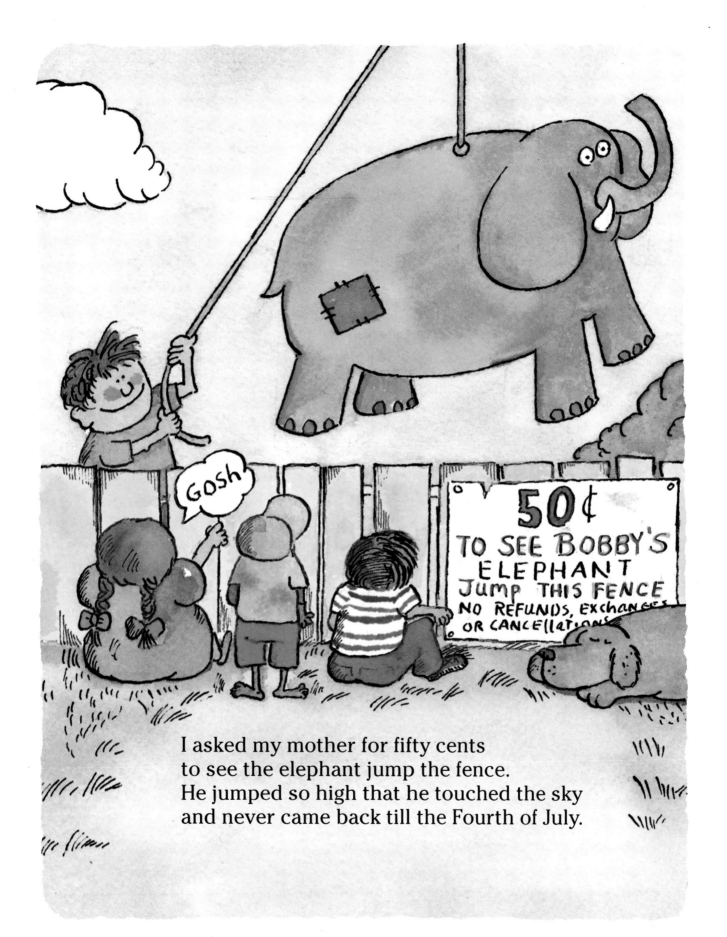

I asked my mother for fifty cents
to see the elephant jump the fence.
He jumped so high that he touched the sky
and never came back till the Fourth of July.

Teddy Bear, Teddy Bear,
turn around.
Teddy Bear, Teddy Bear,
touch the ground.
Teddy Bear, Teddy Bear,
show your shoe.
Teddy Bear, Teddy Bear,
that will do.